The Lost Islander

The Lost Islander

Zach Benard

First Edition

For more information about ThatLitPress and its
publications, please visit **ThatLitSite.com**

Edited by Jayme Karales
Cover art and design by Zach Benard
Interior design by Joel Amat Güell

The Lost Islander
Copyright 2015 by Zach Benard
ISBN: 0988643235
ISBN-13: 978-0-9886432-3-9

Table of Contents:

Where Is My Light? 7
Matching the Sun 9
Palms in the Water 10
A Blend of Hues 11
An Endlessness 12
Oceanic Dreams 13
By the Moon 14
The Current 16
The Lost Islander 18
Sinking Feeling 20
Native Tongue 22
Low Howls 23
The Ebb 25
Dear Home 26
Cold Side 27
Foreign, Part I 28
Foreign, Part II 30
Every Rotation 31
Goodbye, Riptide 33
The House 34
The Vermillion Inside 36
The Elysian Coast 37
The Bottom of the Sea 39
Prints in the Sand 40
The Cool of the Evening 41

Where Is My Light?

The wind carried you away
The salty air left a bitter taste
That matched the feeling in my heart
But you are not to blame

One woman
All I need
You are my light
And I watched
As you faded away through the haze
And out of my sight
But never out of my mind

I'll have left before you know
There's no use
In finding a place to rest
My feet
My arms
My thoughts
They will all stay in motion
Until they meet their end

Enough time has passed
Without you
And enough time has passed
With you
To know that I must be on my way
To you

You are my light that will never go out
My shimmering glory
My radiant wonder
I will set out to find you
You told me your destination
And that will be my destination, too.

Matching the Sun

Together we blossomed
Into a fresh garden
That could survive the seasons
As the leaves hardened
Through vibrancy and growth
Our petals would reach the sky
Matching the sun
For the brightness of its shine

I want to breathe you in
Like the sweet spring air
And abandon my mind's
Wretched thoughts of despair
This vessel will set sail
And endure every storm in its way
We've planted ourselves in rich soil
Destined to bloom without delay

With our bare hands
We cultivated our land.

Palms in the Water

I placed my palms in the water
With hopes of becoming stronger
But it takes more
Than a little blood and dirt
To be washed away

If the mind doesn't change
Then the blood and dirt never left
They remain a stain on the skin
Inked within

My foggy reflection
Was a true representation
Of what I personally believed
And spiritually, by no means
I'm just unhappy with the results
Of what I've received

The cracks in my hands
Know that I haven't wrestled with more
Than I could handle
These cracks will be met
By blisters and cuts
From the earth I will tread

I am a native to this land
And at the same time
I am from nowhere.

A Blend of Hues

Our feet sway as they hang off the edge
A ripple creates as I lightly touch
And the sun starts to drift below the skyline
The horizon portrays a blend of hues
Wait long enough and you'll see stars align
Eventually the sunrise will diffuse
Bleeding through clouds
Marking a saturated collision
We're born to die
But life doesn't feel temporary
Even when days and nights accelerate
When I'm with you

I'll never believe
That I'll leave this world someday
That this blending of hues
Will occur after I'm dead and gone

I'll never conceive
That your feet will sway alone
That this blending of hues
Will have only one of us as its witness

I'll never believe
That someday I'll leave it.

An Endlessness

The view through this spyglass
Reveals a discouraging endlessness
With no edge of the known

Familiar waters
But simultaneously an unfamiliar world

I've got legs for the sea
And the open shore calls my name
Wherever it may be

I'm eager to rest my bones
I'm eager to call you home.

Oceanic Dreams

When the sun drifts underneath
And the moon commands the sky
My oceanic dreams keep me awake
They are the torch to my mind

I want to play with this fire
I want to get burned
I want to glide below sea level
I want the water to fill my lungs
Only to recover at the very last second

And I want to continue
Until I become accustomed
To the burn and to the water

While the sliver in the sky
Illuminates below
And the constellations illustrate
Images above
They are the last thing I see
While I drift at sea
Before I drift to sleep.

By the Moon

The violet sky turns violent
And the shadows are lurking beneath me
Solid black masses against the blue
Demons dressed in fins
I feel their presence
I see them with every flash from above
As it illuminates the scenery for a moment

They're going to try to pull me
To the ocean floor
To the killing floor
Down in the deep

Dirty clouds and thunderous sounds
Brew nearby
I fear this water while it welcomes me
And haunts me
And rocks me
An unforgiving entity
That will swallow me whole
With its cold and dark mouth

My fears see the light of the night
And they appear effortlessly
A crack in the sky fuels the future ruins
And I am left floating

By the moon, I will swear on my life
That this will not be the end

I fell hard into the ocean
I fell hard for you.

The Current

Currently, the current takes me
Because I never learned
How to properly swim
I grab onto the branches
The whites in my knuckles
Match the whites in the water
A deafening flow
That coaxes me
Downstream
And into the unknown

My arms and legs aren't strong enough
My attempts to break through the waves
Fall short as my strides leave me
In the same initial spot

My blood rushes
Flooding my heart
I never was a good swimmer
And although the water
Has always been a fascination of mine
It isn't fascinating in this fashion
It isn't appealing in this way

I lose grasp
And my body
Becomes one with the water
And then, without will
I become one with the adjacent island
That lies stagnant

My migration has been averted
I have come to a new landing
My carrier and my anticipation
Have been capsized and destroyed.

The Lost Islander

Call me the "islander"
I want to wander
But I'm trapped on this land
And I can't be beside her

I am surrounded by open space
It feels emptier now than it's ever been
I am a stranger to this region
And this region is a stranger to me
I have shown my face
But there is a great unknown
Where I have unwillingly
Presented myself

This journey cannot be continued
Not even as a wayfarer
Or my legs will be engulfed
Along with the rest of my remains

I stare at the radiant sun
Dangling in the blue above
And I wish I could chase the light
Transfixed in front of me
Forever rising and falling
But my feet are trapped
And I won't fall for the bait
To lead me alone into the sea

Like the trees in the forest
Yearning to reach the sky
My desire to escape only grows

But like the trees in the forest
Rooted to the ground
My roots are beginning to form

I only truly know of the world
That I am shown
And that is why I want to navigate
The entirety of the earth.

Sinking Feeling

I used to think
That anywhere beneath the starlit sky
Would be home
But in my naivety
I have seen that I was simply wrong
I am my own anchor

Feathered wings spread
And I live vicariously

My feet remain in the sand
The grains encompass my toes
And will soon build up to my ankles
And with every second
That sinking feeling conquers all

Submerge me
Root me to the land
Along with the rotten, barren trees
And the ghosts
That once roamed
Either willingly or unwillingly
The souls that still wander
Through the dark of the night

The procession of days
The succession of seasons
It will all pass.
And I will be left here
Motionless to the world
Nobody will know of my demise

Has it become my fate to bury my bones
Here on this island?

I've got this sinking feeling in my heart
That I will join them.

Native Tongue

Before I softly settle into the earth
Your native tongue
Lifts me from my roots
And coaxes me
Into the dark of the night
Past the bark of the trees
And the bark of the ghosts
Who haunt my insides

I am led
Through the shadows
Through the cold, dirt path
The esoteric passage
And as I make my way out
Vibrancy fills my vision
The land and the water
The green and the blue
I step on a lush ground
And I see you
Lying in the grass
Waiting for me.

Low Howls

With a step
Onto this lush ground
The earth shook
This mystical dreamscape
Has immediately transformed
Into a bleak wasteland

You evaporated
Into a smoke signal of dismantled intimacy

It was all a mirage
For my eager eyes
Anticipating something
Beyond this world
That could heal my weathered body
I didn't know you would be so volatile

The low howls sound
Muffled by the leaves
But still in my ears
And the contorted branches
Form into a maniacal design

There are faces in the shadows
With jagged edges
It skews my vision
It leaves me retracing my steps
Back to the coast
Where I can reside for now
Underneath the palm trees
In this tropical disaster.

The Ebb

The ebb on the beach
Reminds me of how easily
I can be taken away
Into the dark of the cerulean

An unusually calm disposition for the waves
That normally shatter on the sand

The water moves in rhythms
Like we did

I wish for my lungs to fill
With the essence of your floral aroma
To substitute the salty wall
That is carried through my body

I am jealous of the fins
Forever in motion
My discoveries come up short
For finding a match to your irises
To satiate my desire
To see the same hazel
That I see whenever our eyes meet

With every swell
I yearn for you to appear

I put myself under this duress.

Dear Home

Dear Home,
I know nothing about you anymore
I have become so detached
From your alleged meaning
That you are not concrete to me
You are an empty concept

I want you to be mighty
I want you to contain the wild
I want you to be alive
I want too much
I have an honest heart for you
But the gap is widening
Between what I have
And what I want

My home cannot be pinpointed
It is forever in motion

The fleeting memories of you
Take form
Of a dried up riverbed
A cease in its flow
Until the last drop runs down
Exiting the delta.

Cold Side

Kissing the cold side of your face
It's got me thinking
That maybe this winter weather
Isn't the only thing that creates a distance
Between the warmth of my body to yours

We are two continents drifting apart
Who lost our content
We are two bodies of water
Who have begun our descent
Plunging into the depths
Never to return to the surface
You can taste the water in my lungs
And the salt on my tongue

Can I see the future in my dreams?
Or is it a vivid image
Resonating with haunting tones?
Like the wind in a dark forest
An atmospheric ambience
Where the trees are too tall
And the visibility is too short.

Foreign, Part I

Another entity inhabits this island
A man of my age
Bearded, long-haired
Rugged, tired
A survivor whose hopes
Of an ephemeral stay
Didn't come true

And with hesitation
I remain reserved
We possess different prose
He writes his name in the sand:
Talbot

We communicate through the sand
But difficulty increases
As the storm washes away our words
We go unheard

Complete comprehension is absent
Gestures can only go so far
When this island
Has your hands tied

My almost companion
Cannot understand me

But through our broken words
We agree to help each other
To devote our future
To escaping this land
That has been separated
From the rest of the world.

Foreign, Part II

I awake to a crash of a bolt
And it doesn't surprise me
The dark circles under my eyes
Are here to stay

My eyes adjust
And I can see a trail of faint smoke
Rising to the sky

My exploration ensues
And I step through the cold ground
And when I arrive
My eyes must further adjust

The embers are all that remain
And they provide a soft light
On my almost-companion

He lies dead in the sand
With wide eyes
And stiff limbs
And foreign tongue
He will now roam these parts forever.

Every Rotation

I can feel the world turn
Through every rotation in rhythm
My bones are becoming weary
And the sun is becoming dim
The rivers are flowing faster
The tides are crashing down harder
I am in strange terrain
Unable to adjust

My shoulders are sore
From the constant shrugging
And my jaw aches
From the constant clenching

My tongue is raw
From the constant biting
My head is throbbing
From the constant worrying

The moon casts a shadow on me
A lonely silhouette

I think I will lay my body down
In this unintended grave
Reduce myself to sand and dust
And become one with the dirt
And one with the earth

Lost hope for a lost soul
To be reaped
By the constant state of fear every night
Only to succumb
To myself

I could waltz to the shoreline
To the coldest of liquids
Just before the freezing point
That makes your hairs stand up
On your neck, your arms, your body
And hope, with each step,
That the riptide takes me away.

Goodbye, Riptide

My dreams and thoughts
Have caused enough harm
My ailing mind will surely deteriorate
If I don't leave
So the search begins for anything
Anything at all
Anything that could serve a purpose
To the continuation of this journey
To find her
To match my vision to my thoughts

Scarce resources
Will prove to be worthy
This vessel will come to life
Vindictive against the current

The derelict wooden mammoths
Of this island's past
Will be crafted
Into a makeshift mode of transport

I will leave behind this land
And these disturbing thoughts
I will set sail once again
And I will reach her

Goodbye, riptide.

The House

I hope this is a light that never goes out
It is my guide throughout the night
The intensity increases with every motion
Providing a shimmer near the shore

Magnify this view
So I can perceive
That this yellow shine is not
A fool's goldmine
A cornucopia of false hope
A mirage produced by my mind

My hopes become interstellar
Young stars burning bright
My desired reality is surfacing
With every paddle
With every blink
With every second

As I near the coast
My hopes are fulfilled
My eyes will soon set sight
On your face
Where I will cup my hands
And then wrap my arms around you
Embracing your soft skin
The beat of my heart
A fast tempo

In a moment that I wish would just
Slow
Down.

The Vermillion Inside

I will push forward
Until the vermillion inside of me
Exits my skin
And races down
Leaving a trail
Leaving a part of me
In the wretched depths
Forever beneath me

I will push forward
Until the pain that activates my lungs
Billows from my mouth
An aggressive tone
Melding with the night
As it echoes for nobody
Before it is lost in the void

I will catch you
Before I catch my breath.

The Elysian Coast

I am far from home
The wind carried me to you
To the elysian coast
And the sun has risen
And the storm has passed
And I am at a new home

I've retired from the space of the sea
And now I've reached my ending

You can taste the lightning in me
Electrifying our bones

I am returning from battle
Seven weeks' war
Battle with the ocean
Battle with the mind

I want the birds to sing us to our beds
Where we will bathe in honeysuckle
The rising sun will be our scenery
As I begin a new day
And a new life
And I will see your hazel eyes
That turn gold in the sun

But before our climactic embrace
Before I can feel your soft skin
And your dark, silky hair
Before our eyes match
A slip of the foot
And you're submerged.

The Bottom of the Sea

You were at the bottom of the sea
And I was positioned at the end of the land
The cerulean swallowed your fleeting hand
Stealing my final moments
Of serenity with you

Remember the tropical breeze you felt?
It preceded the surrounding terrors

It wasn't only the water
That had caused you pain
And I felt it vicariously

I had none of you
But now I have all of you
And I was able to retrieve your heart
From the depths of constricting sorrow

We contest against
The embodiment of pawns
We progress towards
The days of halcyon.

Prints in the Sand

You renovated my bitter heart
Into a sweet honey
You livened my feet
As they created prints in the sand
Along with yours
Around the orange of the fire

We moved together in rhythm
Just like the swelling of the tide,
But twice the tempo

We waited until daybreak
To extinguish the physical flames;
But another fire existed
In the chambers of our hearts.

The Cool of the Evening

I have reached my denouement
Of this voyage
The cool of the evening passes
And we are met by the crash
Of the sun over the horizon
Through our periphery
As we stare above

The one I love
Gazes above with me
Unable to sleep
With the fear of time passing
As the clock ticks
And the seconds pass
And all around us
There is a countdown
To the end of the year
To the end of the day
To the end of this moment

However
We shuffle that last one
Straight to the back of our heads
And enjoy the seconds
As they pass us by.

Zach Benard is a filmmaker, writer, photographer, and occasional ukulele player from Massachusetts. He is the creator of several short films and music videos and he has written numerous poems and short stories. He is also a contributing editor for ThatLitSite.

Twitter: @ZachBenard